10 Lessons From The Wonderland

How we can learn Management and Business lessons in daily lives simply by mindful living?

Morti Miscellany

Dedicated to:
All Beloved Animals, Parents, and Young Readers

CONTENTS

PREFACE

If you are reading the free first part of the book (as an option on amazon kindle), and you think you cannot spend money to buy it due to any reason, then you can contact the author on Twitter using direct message (@MortiMiscellany). The author can help you get a free copy during promotions. This offer is valid even if you want to gift a copy to a friend or a young one. The author will not ask you a reason or explanation for anything. You will just get a link to a promotional free copy whenever available. The author firmly believes that all the books in the world should be freely available to those who cannot afford the price for any reason. Unfortunately, this option cannot be utilized for the printed version of the book.

The idea to write this book came up while talking to a young student pursuing the first semester of undergraduate education. We were discussing the importance of management skills and leadership lessons that can prepare people for life. At the end of our discussion, we agreed with the conclusion that a keen observer who lives mindfully, can learn management lessons from everything in the living world. A few of the examples we discussed are partially fictionalized to be included in this book.

The initial purpose was to prepare a children's book. However, by the end of the book, I realized that some of the concepts are too abstract for a child. Hence, the best age group for this book is someone in late adolescence or older person. After reading the book, one of my friends suggested that this book can be a good resource for parents too. It may help the parents to instill critical thinking abilities among their kids.

32 years ago, I was just an infant in the world of human relationships. I spent the last 32 years trying to understand human behavior, psychology, interpersonal skills, relationship management, and management skills. These 32 years taught me one lesson i.e.

"This world is an amazing accident (for an atheist) or creation (for a believer) that presents us with numerous opportunities to learn every day. All we need is a curious mind and a playful heart that can read the encyclopedia kept in this global observatory."

I tried to collect a lot of examples and include them in this book. This was the first book, I ever wrote. I am an amateur writer still learning to put my thoughts in the form of writing. Besides, I learned English communications mainly in 3rd decade of my life. Hence, there are certain language-based limitations that I am still trying to improve. However, I decided to publish it as sometimes we just need to take a step at a time.

There are 11 chapters in this book. I offered it to a few of my friends. All of them said that book chapters gradually become interesting. If you want to read just one chapter, please read Chapter 9. If you want to read 3 chapters, then please read Chapters 9 to 11. Otherwise, please read the entire book. However, I feel if I was a reader, I will enjoy Chapter 9 more than any other chapter.

Most chapters are split into 3 parts. The first part is a story. The second part is an application of the story to real-life based on my or my friend's experiences. The third part includes fun facts that can be very useful for some people and irrelevant for others. Overall, the content is partially fictionalized for the purpose of smoother storytelling. The inspirations for the content came from many real-life events. However, every effort is made to obscure the identity of people involved in inspiring events.

The purpose of this book is to change the way we think about management or leadership lessons. We all use a bunch of these lessons in our everyday life. We all learn them every day. Hence, the purpose is just to ignite that thought and habit to learn from our surroundings.

In short, I tried to design this book for everyone irrespective of age willing to learn a few management lessons while having fun. I will be grateful to get your feedback as reviews or via social media contacts listed at the end of the book. Your feedback will help me become a better writer in the future. In the end, I want to thank you for choosing to read this book out of millions of choices available to book readers.

10 Lessons From The Wonderland

How we can learn Management and Business lessons in daily lives simply by mindful living?

A Short Story Book for Those Who Love to Learn While Having Fun

Written By:

Morti Miscellany

1. INDIVIDUAL

1.1 Short Story 1

The spring has arrived,
And winter is gone!
The sky is clear,
And trees are in bloom!
The city looks beautiful,
With the fresh sunshine!
I have brought home,
A golden friend of mine!

The Old Dinosaur dedicated the above poem to GG

GG was beautiful like sunshine. Its golden color was very attractive. It had black stripes on its body like a tiger. You must be thinking by now:

Who was GG?

The GG was a golden fish and the first friend in the Dinosaur's first personal aquarium. It looked very calm and cool fish at first glance. It was impressively attractive too. The Dinosaur was new to aquarium maintenance. He took all the precautions recommended by experts to provide the best habitat for the GG. One fine day, the Dinosaur decided that the aquarium should be expanded to make it a community tank. The Dinosaur expected that social interaction with other fishes would be good for the GG. In that way, the GG will have few friends as playmates and the groups are always considered more valuable compared to the individual.

The Dinosaur brought home a few more fishes and kept them with the GG. After two days, the Dinosaur found one of the new fish dead. A few days later, one more new fish died. It continued over the next few days and the new fishes kept dying one by one.

The Dinosaur started the analysis of the events. All fishes were young and beautiful. They were healthy too. There was an appropriate quantity as well as the quality of resources (water, food, oxygen, pH, temperature, etc.) required for the healthy living of all the fishes. Most likely, it was not a natural death related to aging, lack of resources, or health issues.

The Dinosaur started active observation of the tank to identify the cause of fish deaths. After a few days of observation, the Dinosaur realized that the GG was acting aggressively with other fishes leading to the injury followed by death for other fishes.

The Dinosaur remembered a management lesson that he had learned earlier in life:

Some people are more valuable to society alone than in a group.

A person who is a great asset alone can become a non-performer or even disruptive in groups.

Every individual has their own quality. The leaders have the ability to identify those individual qualities to bring the best out of every individual.

1.2 Real-Life Management Lesson 1

The team efforts are being publicized across the globe. It has become a custom to promote teamwork and collaboration. Team efforts even have an evolutionary advantage for humans as well as other species. However, some individuals perform best when they work alone. The cause of such individual efficiency may vary. In some cases, the reason could be an early-life adaptation while in other cases it could be related to fear. Depending on the reason, an individual team member can turn out to be a non-performer or a performance disruptor in the team. The leaders must be able to identify where to draw the line to bring the best out of every individual. The leaders should remember:

Keeping an eagle and a horse in the same team does not mean you can claim to have a unicorn.

It will be more productive to think about a way to individually utilize a horse and an eagle than having an imaginary nonfunctional unicorn at the cost of two team members who could be very valuable resources as an individual.

1.3 Fun Facts From Chapter 1

The GG mentioned in the chapter is Gold Gourami. It is a semi-aggressive fish species from the Beta family that do not like to be kept with other colorful fishes. Evolutionarily, they perceive other colorful fishes as a threat to them. They also need a large amount of water per fish. Hence, they are ideal to be kept in a big tank with lots of water.

They like planted aquariums. They will play with plants but never damage the plants. You can keep any immersed or submersed plant with them and both plants, as well as the fish, will act as a happy companion for each other.

Golden gourami is hardy fish. It makes them best for beginner aquarists or kids. It is less demanding compared to most freshwater fishes. They are a little picky about the food though. They like only small flake food made for beta family of fishes. They have a hard-time consuming pellet food as they have a very small mouth. With proper care, the golden gourami can be part of your family for years.

2. DIVERSITY

2.1 Short Story 2

Individual colors are great,
But rainbow need shades!

If the world is unicolored,
It would be quite dull!

The GG was great,
But needed playmate!

Hence, I brought friends,
Who were quite different!

The Old Dinosaur dedicated the above poem to Diversity!

The Dinosaur was happy with GG in the beginning. However, one day while looking at the aquarium, he thought:

"The beauty of nature gets appreciated mainly due to its diversity."

The rainbow cannot be made up of a single color. No matter how important an individual color is in life, it would be dull if it were the only color available in the world. For example, imagine a possibility that every living and non-living object on this planet (or universe) had the same color. The Dinosaur needed to do something to make the aquarium look more diverse.

What did the Dinosaur do to make his home more beautiful?

The Dinosaur decided to prepare a community fish tank. Therefore, he researched for the fish compatibility and brought home seven more friends. Now, the Dinosaur had a total of eight friends from three different species. The Dinosaur knew that the extra family members will need extra space and resources for healthy living. Therefore, the old Dinosaur brought a bigger tank for his new friends.

The Dinosaur's new friends were happy. They had plenty of food supply to eat; plenty of oxygen to breathe, and an optimum amount of light. Everything was going great for a few months. All the fishes were eating well. A healthy eating habit leads to normal development. Four of the Dinosaur’s friends were overeating. They became large and strong. They used to bully the smaller members of the family. They even started eating the food of smaller members of the family. The Dinosaur noticed these changes. The Dinosaur had learned earlier in life:

"Diversity is the most beautiful aspect of a team."

Therefore, he decided not to interfere with the diversity of the group. Few months passed by and the Dinosaur needed to go out-of-station for a week due to some personal work. The Dinosaur set the automatic fish feeder, cleaned the tank, and set-up the filtration system. He had done it during several trips in past and all the tank-mates were fine with this practice in the past. The Dinosaur came back after a week.

Guess what?

Four out of eight fishes in the tank were dead. The two out of four survivors were the weaker ones from two different species in the tank. The larger fishes of the same species had bullied them and did not allow them to feed properly in past. The third and fourth survivors were from a fish species that is an inherently slow eater and slow metabolizer.

The Dinosaur checked everything. He found that

the filter was clogged by the fish food. Probably the food pellets entered the filter and clogged the filtration system. The Dinosaur checked the water quality and found poor quality as the filtration could not clean up the toxicants. The Dinosaur found the reason behind his loss. However, how did the four fishes survive when the stronger ones could not?

The four survivors were the least active fishes. Limiting the activity level helped them maintain low energy needs. Hence, they needed fewer nutrients and less oxygen to survive. Slower metabolism leads to a slower rate of breathing in fishes. Hence, they passed less water through their respiratory system. It helped them minimize their exposure to the toxicants too. Hence, a disadvantage earlier turned out to be an advantage for these fishes. They survived under untenable circumstances where the stronger ones from the group could not survive.

The Dinosaur remembered one more management lesson from his experiences:

Diversity is very important for the long-term performance of the team.

A weaker (less useful) member in regular day to day business can turn out to be a great resource under some unforeseen circumstances.

In short,

A disadvantage now can become an advantage later!

2.2 Real-Life Management Lesson 2

Diversity cannot be emphasized enough in all walks of life. There is a plethora of literature available in the market that emphasizes the diversity of the teams. However, diversity is often limited to race and gender diversity. Race and gender diversity are important as they lead to cultural diversity. If somebody would have asked me 100 years back about diversity, I would have suggested gender and racial diversity. Why? Because in that era we did not have the representation of gender and races. Today some organizations still need to pay attention to gender and racial diversity. However, should we limit ourselves to something basic?

Come on Millennials!

It's time to start a new practice and get a step ahead.

If we want to get a step ahead, we first need to ensure that requirements for racial and gender diversity are met. If we cannot meet that basic step, how could we think about the advanced steps?

Next, we should try to ensure the diversity of thoughts, and experiences. A friend in a management role once told me that he prefers to hire people who will be able to party with him. While doing so he does his best to maintain gender and racial diversity in his team. Many managers use this philosophy for hiring. That is the reason behind subjective bias in hiring.

Considering the psychology behind human relationships. People party with like-minded people. If the last sentence is true, then the managers mentioned in the last paragraph will only hire other like-minded people. Oftentimes, these new hires will be someone who has walked a similar path as the hiring managers. Such teams are easier to manage as the manager can easily predict the behavior of his subordinates.

Now, let us consider that a difficult project/situation comes. This team of like-minded people might think in the same way increasing the possibility that either many or none will come up with a solution. If the former is the case, it is great as the team can unanimously devise a plan to solve the issue. However, what if the situation is quite difficult? There are good chances that none of the teammates would be able to come up with a good solution as all of them will end up thinking the same way. The more experienced member (manager) who could not solve the problem was thinking that way too. Will it solve the problem? Probably, not!

How could the managers have increased the probability of finding a solution?

The answer is simpler. By hiring a diverse team from different races, gender, continents, who could think differently under critical conditions. In this way, diversity of the team can help the organization improve its efficiency too. A diverse team thinks differently in difficult situations increasing the probability of finding a solution. Cultural diversity is important provided it is backed up by the diversity of thoughts and experiences. It will be less useful to have a culturally diverse team of 10 people who think in the same way as other members of the team.

2.3 Fun Facts From Chapter 2

Community tanks are the hardest to maintain aquariums. The community means diversity. It is easier to keep multiple members of the same species of fish. If someone wants to keep multiple species/subspecies of fishes together, he/she must consider multiple factors. Different species have different requirements for food, temperature, water salinity, water pH, space, light, etc. Apart from habitat, aggressiveness is another major factor. Few species of fish are more aggressive compared to others. Some fishes are aggressive only towards a particular species while being compatible with other species. All these factors must be considered before planning a community tank.

Community tanks are not something for beginners. However, beginners usually are more attracted to community tanks due to the beauty of diversity. There is a variety of online resources available to guide the aquarists in preparation for the community tank. Multiple resources should be utilized to decide about the most compatible fish species for the community tank and minimize the error due to the writer's bias.

3. THREAT

3.1 Short Story 3

Diversity means a group of organisms that differs in their characteristics. The last chapter covers the inherent advantage of diversity. Let us now move on to an inherent disadvantage of diversity.

As mentioned in the last two chapters, the Dinosaur decided to bring more fishes and keep it with golden gourami fish (GG) in the tank. When the Dinosaur brought more fishes, he noticed something significant in the tank. He observed that the GG started to chase a few specific fishes. The GG used to chase them continuously until they hide in some less lit part of the tank. The GG did not allow them to eat or rest. Those specific fishes got weaker day by day. They looked highly stressed all the time.

The Dinosaur tried to identify the reason behind GGs behavior. Earlier the GG used to be a very calm fish. What happened suddenly that changed its behavior? The Dinosaur started careful observation. The Dinosaur realized that the GG was only chasing the brighter or more colorful members of each variety (species) while forgiving the less bright or dull or dark-colored fishes. The Dinosaur had learned about species compatibility earlier. However, this case was unusual. The GG had aggressive behavior towards one fish while being friendly to the other fish of the same variety. The Dinosaur decided to research the GG's behavior.

The Dinosaur searched all the available information and found something amusing. The GG is a bright-colored fish. The male gourami often considers other bright color fish as a threat to them. Therefore, they try to chase them out of gourami's territory. It was interesting as the GG did not have any real threat from other fish species. The other fish species used to eat only plant-based food and they were smaller in size too. They were not supposed to compete for mates either. However, there was no way it could be explained to the GG. The GG was only acting based on its instincts that it had inherited from its ancestors.

Anyway, the Dinosaur wanted to find out the solution for this problem as he could not see other fishes stressed. The Dinosaur could not find any information related to solving this problem. There was nothing that could help the Dinosaur to find out a solution. However, the Dinosaur decided that he should not give up.

Did Dinosaur's perseverance pay off?

Let us see. A few days later, the Dinosaur was sitting in front of the fish tank. He realized that the GG was not chasing anyone in the tank. The GG looked calm. Also, other fishes including the bright ones were roaming around freely. Suddenly, the Dinosaur realized that he forgot to turn on the fish tank light that morning. Like all animals, fishes needed a light-dark (day-night) cycle for healthy living. The Dinosaurs used to turn-off the light every evening and turn it back on in the morning. However, he forgot to turn it on that morning. Anyway, the Dinosaur turned the lights on. He was happy with the friendly nature that the GG showed that day. Hence, he decided to continue observing them for some more time.

Guess what?

The GG again started chasing the brighter fishes once the light turned on. It did not take long for the Dinosaur to realize that the bright light makes fishes even brighter. Probably the GG finds them more threatening in bright light. The Dinosaur immediately switched the lights off again. He brought some subdued light bulbs (bulbs that produce a very low amount of light) and fixed them with the aquarium. The Dinosaur was excited as it solved the problem. He kept observing fishes for the next few weeks. All the fishes were living peacefully with each other.

The Dinosaur learned the following management lesson from the event:

Diversity is an asset if you utilize it well,

but it becomes a liability if you fail to invest the time and resources to bring the best out of it.

3.2 Real-Life Management Lesson 3

Management and leadership skills are an important component of someone's corporate success. A great leader or manager is an asset to the business. Therefore, every business should actively invest the time and resources to prepare future leaders. Unfortunately, very few firms like to invest in the development of managerial and leadership skills. However, they are still promoting people based on tenure. These promotions often lead to filling the roles that need managerial or leadership skills but the employee filling the position lack those skills due to a lack of proper training.

In long run, the situation sometimes leads to a toxic work environment where the managers consider their knowledgeable or more experienced subordinates as a threat. Due to lack of proper training, they are afraid to hire someone who has better abilities than the hiring manager. They use fear and threat in managing their subordinates. They threaten the subordinates with punishments, but they lack the ability to reward them for their success. They do not take the blame for their own mistakes and always look for scapegoats for their own failure. They do not have the ability or intention to nurture the talent in the team. They would rather be happy with less skillful but submissive subordinates. This situation is rare but still present in the corporate world.

In long run, this practice hurts only the business itself. Threat from managers affects the productivity of employees. As a human, employees need time to relax and plan. Few occasional high-pressure situations are acceptable as they may sometimes even lead to increased productivity. However, the leaders should avoid a continuously threatening environment that will reduce the productivity of individual employees as well as the revenue of the business itself. Identifying the problem is the first step towards solving it. Hence, one must realize that the issue exists before expecting things to change. Also, if a leader finds such an environment in a company that just hired that leader, then the leader must work hard to change the situation. In my view:

Leaders should be aggressive, energetic, knowledgeable, and hardworking but they also need to be passionate and supportive of their subordinates.

3.3 Fun Facts From Chapter 3

Most pets we keep in our home are directly related to their ancestors who evolved for thousands of years in the wilderness. Multiple factors affected this evolution of the species that includes the availability of food, shelter, mates, environmental conditions, predators present in the area, seasonal variations, etc. The species we see today have survived through various conditions and became the best fit for surviving under those often-untenable conditions. This evolution has resulted in several innate behavioral patterns that are inherited continuously in the species. These innate behaviors are often called instincts or animal instincts.

The animal instincts are pretty accurate about predicting few events that directly affect a particular animal's survival. One can find the logic behind a particular instinct by looking at conditions where that species evolved and survived. These instinctual behaviors are widely studied in laboratories for few species. It is easy to find many such examples online and it is out of the scope of this book to discuss those behaviors. However, these behaviors are often related to food, mating, and avoiding the threat. In short, those instinctual behaviors evolved to ensure the maximum chances of survival for the individual and the species.

4. INSECURITY

4.1 Short Story 4

Sky or seashore,
None are insecure!
People will follow us,
If we become enormous!

The Old Dinosaur dedicated above stanza to the Leadership!

In the last two chapters, the Dinosaur explained the importance of diversity for the survival of the group followed by an inherent disadvantage of diversity. Let us extend the discussion further by talking about other aspects that we did not elaborate on in chapter 2:

What really killed the stronger fishes in the group?

Just to remind you, the fishes that died were the fittest and strongest ones from two species while the weaker ones survived.

HOLD ON FOR A MOMENT!

Didn't we learn in the biology class the Darwinian theory of evolution? Didn't we learn that only those survive who are the fittest in the group? Didn't we extrapolate this theory to the management and business world noting numerous examples showing that the strongest and fittest ones are also the most successful ones?

Does it mean that the Survival of Fittest Theory failed in this case?

No, it did not. The stronger fishes were fittest for survival under normal circumstances but had disadvantage in the toxic environment as explained in chapter 2.

Let us take our observation a step further. To do this, we may have to move a few steps back first. Let us start from a time when all fishes were alive. The Dinosaur observed that the strong fishes used to dominate the weaker fishes and ate all their food too. They also bullied the weaker fishes at times. Aren't the stronger and more experienced fishes supposed to act as leaders?

The fishes in the above examples were insecure. They could not trust other members of the group. They did not invest time in strengthening the other members of the group. They preferred other members of the team to remain weak as it would help the former dominate later. They became a little selfish towards self-interest over group interests. Finally, this insecurity pushed them to a disadvantage when unforeseen circumstances developed in the tank due to an accident.

The filter did not function well as it got accidentally clogged. Larger fishes continued consuming a whole lot of food. The oxygen level in the tank reduced due to inefficient filtration. However, the stronger fishes needed more oxygen compared to smaller fishes to compensate for higher metabolic needs. The toxicant levels increased in their body over hours. It led to the failure of their body function. The Dinosaur lost four friends in this accident.

Few months passed after the above incidence. The Dinosaur observed that the remaining four fishes from the last tank grew well over the last few months. They looked healthy and strong. However, those four fishes were from three different species. As a scientist, the Dinosaur knew that everyone prefers a companion from the same species. Considering this factor and the size of the fishes, the Dinosaur brought home a fish tank that was approximately 7 times larger than his first tank. He also brought few more fishes from each species.

The Dinosaur was happy that each fish had a companion. However, he was worried that his new friends might get distressed if the older fishes start bullying them. Due to this concern, the Dinosaur started carefully observing the fish tank.

Guess what?

The Dinosaur realized that his new friends are too small to eat large pellet food. The Dinosaur now remembered that he had another brand of smaller pellet food earlier. However, as the four large fishes grew, he started buying larger pellet food. At the time, when the Dinosaur brought new smaller fishes, he forgot to bring the smaller pellet for them. The Dinosaur must be getting older. Isn't it?

The Dinosaur decided that he will bring the smaller pellet next time he visits the supermarket. While all these thoughts were going on in the old Dinosaur's mind, he observed something amazing.

Unbelievable!

The larger fishes were breaking down the larger pellets and giving them to the younger ones. The Dinosaur changed his mind. He now wanted to observe this unique behavior. He continued feeding the larger pellets to the fishes and observed fishes for thirty minutes after adding pellets to the tank. The larger fishes continued breaking larger pellets to the smaller ones to feed the new younger friends.

Few days after the incidence, the Dinosaur observed that the younger fishes started following the larger fishes as if the larger one is their leader. It continued over time. Several months later, the smaller fishes themselves grew to become beautiful healthy adults. However, they continued treating the older fish like their leader.

Probably observing the demise of bullies turned the young weaklings from *chapter 2* into successful leaders of this chapter. OR probably cohabiting with selfish people early in life taught them the importance of altruism and this altruistic behavior helped them become a true leader later in life.

The Dinosaur remembered a very important management lesson:

The insecurity and selfishness kill the individual's potential to become a leader.

Compassion and helping others are the natural qualities of true leaders.

One can become stronger temporarily and climb few steps by hurting the interests of the subordinates or colleagues in the team. However, one must help others to take a leap of success in the realm of leadership.

4.2 Real-Life Management Lesson 4

The corporate ladder has become the definition of leadership these days. People have started confusing supervisory roles with leadership. The promotion to supervisory roles is governed by the number of years one spends in the organization or similar businesses. People start claiming themselves leaders once they get supervisory roles. However, the supervisory roles or managerial roles do not make you a leader.

You can differentiate the leaders from managers by asking three simple sets of questions i.e.

1. *Why is another person following Mr. /Mrs. /Ms. XYZ? Are they following them only for material benefits such as employment, promotion in the same organization, recommendation for getting a job in a different organization, getting business, or some other potential benefit?*

2. *Do people get inspiration from Mr. /Mrs. /Ms. XYZ? Do they have a true sense of respect for Mr. /Mrs. /Ms. XYZ?*

3. *Will the respect for Mr. /Mrs. / Ms. XYZ will remain the same*

way even if the follower does not get the direct or indirect material benefits?

If someone gets the response of 'Yes' for all three of the above set of questions, then that person is a true leader provided that the response provided is honest and not tempered for potential benefits. However, if someone gets one or more 'No' in the response, then that person might be merely a supervisor or manager with a lack of true leadership skills.

With the increasing unemployment and competitive job markets, many managers have become insecure. One of my friends was threatened to be fired just because he had knowledge close to someone with a managerial role. Just to mention the exact statement, the feedback was as follows:

"Mr. X we know you have great knowledge due to your background. All the answers you gave were right. However, we do not want you to answer scientific questions related to this project as your role does not require you to answer this question. Someone 3 levels above you (where Mr. X will reach after 3 promotions) has the responsibility to answer those scientific queries."

Wait! Are you kidding? First, the manager accepted that Mr. X is knowledgeable enough to answer the scientific queries. It means that the manager accepted that Mr. X is someone who has knowledge equivalent to a managerial role. However, Mr. X was threatened that he will be fired if he answers the scientific questions as it is not a requirement in his job responsibility.

Not to mention, Mr. X was fired 2 weeks later by the same manager on the ground of non-performance. Yes, it is a true incidence. Similar incidences have occurred in several organizations. I leave it up to the reader to decide whether Mr. X was a non-performer or a person with a high level of skills.

There are managers who clearly say that they do not want to hire someone who can quickly climb the corporate ladder to replace them. This insecurity makes the organizations lose many good candidates who could have made a substantial difference for the organization.

Here comes the difference between manager and leader. If there was a leader in the shoe of Mr. X's manager, the leader would have helped Mr. X get few quick promotions. The leader could have utilized it as an example of his ability to help subordinates grow in life and professional abilities. It could have helped the leader himself get a higher up role in the organization helping the leader (manager) himself/herself.

In short, the manager's insecurity resulted in a loss for the organization, Mr. X as well as the manager himself/herself. If the manager would have not been insecure, he/she could have helped everyone including himself/herself. One should always remember:

The leaders are aggressive, energetic, fast-paced, and intelligent individuals who are not insecure or selfish because insecurity and selfishness are the biggest enemies of leadership abilities.

4.3 Fun Facts From Chapter 4

Charles Robert Darwin was a passionate naturalist who was born in a wealthy family. His father wanted him to become a physician, but he decided to pursue his passion and explore nature. Darwin traveled around the world for 5 years observing different species. Darwin published his observations in '*The Voyage of the Beagle*' in 1839. He also published several other interesting books throughout his life i.e. *On the Origin of Species by Means of Natural Selection* (1859), *The Variation of Animals and Plants under Domestication* (1868), *The Descent of Man and Selection in Relation to Sex* (1871), *The Expression of the Emotions in Man and Animals* (1872), *The Power of Movement in Plants* (1880), and *The Formation of Vegetable Mould through the Action of Worms with Observations on their Habits* (1881). His work mainly covered the evolutionary theories indicating that all the species evolved from common ancestors through the process of natural selection. The Darwinian Evolutionary theory of natural selection was later rephrased as '*Survival of the Fittest Theory*' by Herbert Spencer i.e. an English Philosopher.

Herbert Spencer was a great intellectual who was a biologist, economist, anthropologist, and sociologist. He had coined the term '*Survival of the Fittest*' as a theory of economics and presented it in correlation with Darwin's theory of natural selection. Darwin later adopted the phrase in his later book to replace 'natural selection'.

Due to the reasons mentioned in the last paragraph, the 'Survival of the Fittest' theory has become part of the curriculum in evolutionary biology as well as the business schools. In my view, it is one of the best theories that describe the chances of success based on the diversity of the group (business or species). However, diversity means multi-talented groups in the business world.

5. EFFECT

5.1 Short Story 5

The old Dinosaur was happy with the diversity of his fishes. His aquarium made him passionate about fishes. Being a scientist and keen observer, the Dinosaur always liked to try something new and find out the reasons behind every event. The Dinosaur believed:

This universe and everything in nature is connected by a cause-effect relationship. If something has happened, then there must be a cause behind it. Also, if one does something then it must have some effect.

The Dinosaur must be old and lunatic to think that way. Isn't it?

Let us see what happens next. The Dinosaur had quite a good variety of fish. Still, he developed a fresh passion for a variety of goldfish. Therefore, he did some research and prepared a large aquarium to bring home goldfishes. While deciding about goldfish the Dinosaur found a dozen of varieties of goldfish. All the pet stores in the town had at least 2-3 different varieties of goldfish. They were available at very economic prices too.

The Dinosaur was an avid traveler. He had traveled thousands of miles in his life, but he had never seen a single goldfish in the wilderness.

Weird! Isn't it?

What made goldfish so abundant in the pet stores but so rare in the wilderness? Based on the Dinosaur's belief mentioned at the beginning of this chapter, the Dinosaur decided that there must be a cause behind the current state of goldfish existence.

Being a scientist, the Dinosaur started researching the origin of goldfish. The information mentioned in the next paragraph is the information Dinosaur found from his research. This information is available at several places on the internet. The Dinosaur just summarized the available information into the following sentences. The reader should feel free to refer to other resources:

"The Goldfish is a variety of species that came into existence from some genetic changes in the carp fishes in eastern Asia and China. The people of China started domesticating the genetically changed (mutated) forms as they looked beautiful. Over roughly a thousand years of domestication and selective breeding lead to an abundance of goldfish in pet stores as they are very popular pets. However, in the wilderness, the mutated species did not have any survival advantage over the wild variety. Therefore, it did not multiply to a great extent in the wilderness."

It was an exciting finding for the Dinosaur. He had read somewhere that human civilization had increased the chance of survival for many animal/ plant species while making a few others extinct. However, the Dinosaur was excited to find a new example.

The Dinosaur continued keeping goldfish. He started collecting different varieties of goldfish. However, Dinosaur wondered for all this time why the goldfish were called goldfish because he had found goldfishes of only red and other colors. Why would someone call a fish goldfish if it is not golden (yellowish/tan) in color? One fine day, the Dinosaur found a goldfish that was of real gold (yellowish/tan) color. However, Dinosaur realized that these particular-colored goldfish are rare. The Dinosaur again did research and found out the answer mentioned in the next paragraph:

"The golden (yellowish/tan) colored goldfish were forbidden for the public. It was the color that only imperial family could have at one point in time. This led to the abundance of other colored goldfishes".

After learning about the goldfishes and their history the Dinosaur confirmed a group of lessons that he had learned earlier in life as a budding scientist and a student:

Every event in the world is associated with an amazing cause-effect cascade.

If there is a problem, there must be another event that is causing the problem.

It is important to identify the cause to solve the problem.

The careful observation and logical thinking are the best tools to identify the cause of a problem.

5.2 Real-Life Management Lesson 5

The managers in different industries often need to identify the cause of the problem to minimize the future possibility of facing the same problems again. Logical analysis and careful observation are important for this purpose. The same applies to problem-solving in our everyday life. Sometimes it is required to move few steps back to make an effective observation. Doing some research is another way of solving a problem. Oftentimes, the problems we face are ones faced by someone else already in past. Probably they identified a solution and kept some record. If we can access those records, then we can get our solution. The internet is a great tool for this purpose.

5.3 Fun Facts From Chapter 5

Goldfish are one of the most popular fish across the world. There are rarely any kids who go to the fish section of a pet store and come back without noticing one or another variety of goldfish. Even after being so popular, there are many misconceptions around goldfish keeping. Many amateur aquarists keep goldfish in bowls as it is seen in many advertisements and movies. However, goldfish are a species that needs plenty of water. They produce a lot of ammonia. They get stressed if kept in limited water like bowls. Aquarists should make sure that the goldfish gets 5-10 gallons of water per fish. Younger (1-2 months old) fishes are okay with less water though.

The shorter memories of goldfish are another misconception about goldfish. They can be trained for some behavioral activities. This is not possible if goldfish truly had a shorter memory span. If an aquarist finds ways to interact with goldfish, they will be able to easily deny the myth of their shorter memories.

6. COLLABORATION

6.1 Short Story 6

Water was amazing,
As the first source
of living!
The land increased the beauty,
By increasing
the diversity!

The Old Dinosaur dedicated above stanza to the terrestrial animals!

The last few chapters covered the stories of fishes and aquariums. If the Dinosaur could learn so much from fishes that were living in the limited-sized aquarium. The Dinosaur wondered

How much could the Dinosaur learn from the terrestrial animals?

Considering this question, the Dinosaur brought home a group of guinea pigs as new friends. They were all young and beautiful when they joined the family. The Dinosaur had picked the guinea pigs of different age groups from different stores. It helped him ensure a higher genetic as well as phenotypic diversity among them. All the guinea pigs were anxious for the first few days as they came to a new place and met new friends. The Dinosaur allowed them to get acquainted with each other and the environment for few weeks. The Dinosaur provided regular food and water to the group. After a month, the Dinosaur started to observe their interesting behavioral characteristics.

First, the Dinosaur started introducing them to the new places in the home. Whenever the Dinosaur kept the group in a new place, the group stayed together for some time, and then the adults will start to explore the area while the younger members of the group will stay at the same place. Once the adults make sure that the area is safe, they made a peculiar noise/sound, and then the rest of the group would start exploring the area. They also preferred who would explore the area first. Every time, the same guinea pig (*the explorer*) used to go to explore the area first. The Dinosaur first thought that it is just based on convenience. Therefore, he tried putting the explorer in the center of the group.

However, the guinea pigs used to make way for the explorer to come out and explore the area first to ensure that it is safe.

Surprising! Isn't it?

The Dinosaur next tried changing the food. He started giving them more green vegetables and less pellet food. For some reason, they all loved green vegetables. One day, the Dinosaur only gave them pellet food. He expected them to consume pellet food without any issue as they used to consume it in past. However, it did not happen. The younger ones in the group started making noise looking towards the Dinosaur. The Dinosaur went near them. They used their head to point towards the food bowl. The Dinosaur observed that the adult guinea pigs were not eating either. However, only younger ones made noise and pointed towards the food bowl. The Dinosaur gave them green vegetables and all guinea pigs enjoyed it together.

One day, a wild cat somehow entered the Dinosaur's place. She tried to attack the guinea pigs. Suddenly, the older guinea pigs became defensive. They formed a shield around the younger ones in the group. The younger guinea pigs wanted to come closer to the cat, but the older guinea pigs somehow realized the threat and forbid the younger ones. The older guinea pigs together attacked the cat. Finding herself surrounded by three guinea pigs, the cat ran away.

It was an amazing collaboration that the Dinosaur got to observe among the guinea pigs. The Dinosaur tested each event by trying to repeat it by presenting similar situations and the same guinea pigs acted each time in the same way. The cat invasion event was replicated by the dinosaur using a soft toy resembling the cat. However, the behavior was again recreated by three older guinea pigs. The Dinosaur learned another management lesson:

Everyone has unique characteristics that are usually quite different compared to others in groups.

If every person needs to do everything then each one in the group will be exhausted and productivity will be affected.

Collaborations among the individuals help the group by increasing the productivity by facilitating better utilization of the time and resources.

6.2 Real-Life Management Lesson 6

Collaborations have become an essential part of almost every profession. It was very common in the 19th and 20th centuries to see an expert working in multiple domains without any collaboration with any other expert. For example, a simple google search will lead you to find many experts who were a philosopher, a political theorist, a biologist, and an economist, etc. at the same time. However, it is very uncommon to see such a personality in the 21st century.

We live in a fast-paced world, where expertise in one domain is valued more than being the jack of all trades. Hence, collaborations among the experts of different fields have become essential to make any major discovery or progress in any direction. Few exceptions can still be found but there are exceptions to almost every theory.

Considering the importance of collaborations in today's world, it becomes essential for the leaders and the managers to identify the best collaborative potential. As a human, we all have biases. However, we must take utmost care to avoid the ill-effects of those biases on our future productivities.

One of my colleagues was an excellent researcher in his field. He liked to collaborate only with the researchers from a particular geographic area in Asia. That colleague might have some social level of comfort working with people from that geography. However, it affected the success of a research project that had excellent potential. Probably that project could have been more successful if the aforementioned researcher would have collaborated with some other experts without giving consideration to the geographical origin of the particular researcher. There are numerous other examples where researchers/managers try to limit their collaborations to a particular institute (often their home institute)/group/geographical area/race. At least a few of such collaborations could have been more fruitful if the managers could come out of their own comfort zone to explore the expertise of people from other institutes/geographic origin/group/race.

Everybody understands the importance of collaboration in today's world. However, while identifying the collaborative potential a leader/manager should come out of their comfort zone and keep the best interest of the project in mind without letting the personal biases take over the institutional/business interests. Coming out of our comfort zones is a minimal requirement for great collaboration.

Coming out of our comfort zones is a minimal requirement for great collaboration.

6.3 Fun Facts From Chapter 6

Scientific theories suggest that life evolved in the sea. First, the small molecules were converted into more complex macromolecules. Then those macromolecules came together to form the first simple form of life. These simple forms evolved to become aquatic multicellular organisms. Later those multicellular organisms evolved further to form terrestrial organisms including the human being.

Thousands of macromolecules work together for the proper functioning of life. A simple movement of our fingers involves collaborations among thousands of cells. Each of those cells could exist itself because of the collaborations among proteins, lipids, DNA, carbohydrates, etc. In my view:

Life is nothing but an excellent collaboration among the thousands of macromolecules.

Life cannot exist in the absence of these collaborations. Also, collaborations will not have any importance in the absence of life.

Several animal species (e.g., ants, birds, and humans) evolved to live in social structures which are again the collaborative models created by multicellular species to increase the chances of the survival of those species. The ecosystems are collaborations among several species to form a stable environment for the best possibility for survival of all those species in an area for years. It is out of the scope of this book to mention all those collaborations. However, disturbing any of these collaborations affect the entire system. For example, disturbance to macromolecules in the body often leads to diseases. Similarly disturbing the existence of a particular species affects the entire ecosystem. There are several excellent resources on the internet for a more elaborate understanding of these collaborations. I just want to emphasize:

Collaborations are the basis of life.

7. LIMITS

7.1 Short Story 7

The universe is a summit,
The sky is not a limit!
Beyond a certain time,
The limits are only in our mind!

Dedicated to the human mind!

Impressed by the guinea pigs mentioned in the last chapter, the Dinosaur decided to bring another species of terrestrial animals. This time, the Dinosaur brought home a group of young and beautiful rabbits. For the safety of young rabbits, the Dinosaur prepared a barn with tall wooden walls. The rabbits were free to play and roam around within the barn, but they could not jump over it.

The purpose of the barn was to keep rabbits together when they are young. This will ensure their safety and growth till they are able to defend themselves in case they are confronted by another animal. The barn included a small home for rabbits where they could sleep and hide along with a grassy area for them to play. When they were young, the rabbits used to try to jump over the wall of the barn. However, they could not climb the wall. They used to try to find other ways to get out of the barn. However, they remained unsuccessful in their attempts to get out of the barn.

Three months passed and all rabbits turned out to be beautiful adult rabbits. They looked strong enough to defend themselves and fast enough to run and hide in case of an unforeseen difficult situation. On one weekend, the Dinosaur opened the barn for rabbits so that they could explore the surrounding area and play more openly. Surprisingly, none of the rabbits tried to get out of the barn. The Dinosaur left the barn's door open and started observing rabbits from a distant site. The rabbits came one by one and looked out of the door. Then, they went back to play in the barn. It was surprising that none of the rabbits crossed the boundaries of the barn even when the doors of the barn remained open for several days.

At this point, the Dinosaur decided to play an active role. He went to the barn and picked two of the rabbits. He brought them out of the barn and kept them at some distance from the barn. They played outside for few minutes and then went back to the barn. The next day, the Dinosaur repeated it. This time they played outside for a little longer and went back to the barn. Once they entered the barn, the Dinosaur closed the door. The Dinosaur opened the barn's door the following day to again bring the rabbits out. However, this time the two rabbits themselves walked slowly and carefully towards the door. The Dinosaur did not interfere and kept observing. Within few minutes those two rabbits went out of the barn. Other rabbits from the group followed the first two rabbits. Within few days, all the rabbits started freely exploring the area outside the barn. If you remember, their earlier attempts to go out at early age had failed. Probably that is why they had stopped trying. The positive role played by the Dinosaur made them realize that the original limitations are gone. Hence, they started exploring the area. The Dinosaur learned an important management lesson from this event:

Something that did not work in past does not mean that it will never work.

Sometimes we accept our defeat and stop trying even though new avenues are clearly visible.

The leaders must sometimes play an active role to remind the team about their potential and inform them about the new avenues. Things start falling in place once the team realizes its potential.

7.2 Real-Life Management Lesson 7

As humans, we are all dependent on modeling in some way. From scientists to managers, everyone tries to solve problems by utilizing examples from the past. We try to create a dataset of past events, set the event-descriptors, and try to simulate future problems in the existing dataset to predict the best solutions for our problems. As managers, it is good to utilize these references as it will minimize the risk for the business. However, we should be cautious in claiming that something will not work in your favor for the eleventh time because it did not work that way for the last ten times or vice versa.

The leaders are those who try to fit problems (new or old) in a new paradigm and try to design a fresh approach to solve them. Modeling can keep us running at the same pace, but we will always need a new approach to take a leap. We cannot use a car model to fly a plane without adding wings or some other physical levitating force with it. In the same way, one cannot take a business from number fifty to number one by doing the same things that one did for ten previous years unless the other 49 businesses close overnight. In short:

A new paradigm and a fresh approach are the best way to overcome persisting limitations.

7.3 Fun Facts From Chapter 7

Rabbits are very friendly and highly energetic pets. They like to eat a variety of vegetables. They are very fond of carrots. Young kids love the rabbits. In recent decades, more and more people started feeding the fatty pellet food available in pet stores. It somehow makes them overweight and lazy. In this way, it becomes easier to play with the rabbits. However, they are more fun if they are fed a natural diet e.g., grass, leafy vegetables, carrots. They also love cookies that have low or no sugar. They drink plenty of water every day. In short, they love to eat healthy vegetable-based foods.

The rabbits older than 1-year can be toilet trained. They are clean freaks and love to live in clean habitats. They have a curious mind that makes them an explorer. Their sleeping pattern varies based on their comfort. They sit and rest in a small area if they are afraid. They like to spread their body as much as they can and rest if they feel that the surrounding is safe. Last but most important, they sleep on their back with all four legs in the air if they feel completely safe. The last one is a rare sight. However, the day you observe this position, you can be pretty sure that your rabbits consider you a friend that they can trust.

8. STATISTICS

8.1 Short Story 8

In the last chapter, you read about the limitations and modeling. Hence, it makes sense to move next to an essential component of the modeling i.e. statistics. Let us discuss the Dinosaur's experience with the statistics.

Being a scientist by profession, the Dinosaur had a habit of defining possibilities based on statistics. However, nature is full of surprises and a great surprise was waiting for the Dinosaur at his home. The Dinosaur had a great group of pets at home for quite some time. Animal activists across the world usually recommend making the pets infertile by either neutering the male or spaying the female. In this way, the animal activists try to ensure that none of the pet animals or their offspring is abandoned by the pet owner. The pets usually seen in human society are the ones who are bred to live with humans. They have adapted for generations for this purpose. Usually if abandoned, these pets are not able to survive on their own for a long time in the wild. Hence, the animal activists do a great job to ensure humane treatment of our pets that are more important than family members for many people.

The Dinosaur decided that he is willing to take the responsibility of breeding and taking care of the offspring of one or more of his pets. As all the terrestrial males he had were neutered, he decided to breed the fishes. The Dinosaur had a total of 10 fishes from three different varieties (species) living in two different tanks. The smaller tank had 4 fishes (2 Gold Gourami, and 2 Black Molly). Each of these couples had one male and one female. It was not something unusual. The Dinosaur had learned that if someone has two pets, there are approximately 50% chances that they will be of the opposite gender (i.e. 25% chance of both being male, 25% chance of both being female, and 50% chance of one being male and other beings female). As the tank was small and there were two species of fish, the Dinosaur decided to breed fishes present in the other tanks.

The second tank was a larger tank that had 6 fishes of the same variety (goldfish). The Dinosaur had never tried to identify their genders earlier. 6 fishes had different color patterns and they were bought from different stores at different times. It made the Dinosaur think that the fish represent random individuals of a diverse population. Due to recent interests in breeding the fishes, the Dinosaur decided that he will identify the gender of each goldfish and then pick a healthy couple to help them breed. The Dinosaur searched online for the characteristics that help the breeders to differentiate the males from females. The Dinosaur made the list of characteristics and watched few videos. The Dinosaur was confident enough that the list of characters and videos were informative enough to identify the gender of his goldfishes.

Guess what was the surprise?

The Dinosaur picked his first goldfish and kept it in a bowl to identify the gender. As per all the criteria that the Dinosaur had listed, this fish was a female goldfish. Isn't that great news? The Dinosaur already found a female who will be able to produce eggs for breeding. He just needed to identify a male fish that will help to fertilize the eggs. The Dinosaur got very excited.

The Dinosaur picked his second fish and tried to identify its gender. Well! This fish was a female too. That was not a piece of bad news. As per the statistics, if someone has a random population of six pets then there are 50% chances that three of those pets will be females and the other three will be males. Being confident about his scientific training and knowledge of statistics, the Dinosaur thought to identify the gender of the third fish.

Guess What?

The third fish was female too. The Dinosaur was amused at his finding. However, he picked the fourth fish to identify its gender. After careful analysis, the Dinosaur found that even the fourth fish was female. That is great! The Dinosaur had plenty of female options. Also, even one male is enough to fertilize the egg from several female fishes. Due to his training as a scientist and his knowledge of statistics, the Dinosaur knew that if someone has five randomly selected fishes (or pets) then that pet host can be more than 90% confident that at least one of those pets will have gender opposite to the gender of one or more pets in the group. As I mentioned earlier, the Dinosaur had a total of six (means more than five) goldfish. Therefore, he was pretty sure that at least one of the remaining two goldfish should be male.

The Dinosaur picked the fifth fish and characterized it. It was a female too. Let us see statistics. If someone has 6 fishes, then that person can be more than 95% confident that at least one of the fish will have gender opposite to other fishes. With mixed feelings, the Dinosaur checked the last fish, and it was female too.

Something could be wrong.

Probably Dinosaur did not properly differentiate between male and female goldfish. Probably he needed more information to do it correctly.

To confirm his doubt and test his ability, the Dinosaur went to a pet store that sold the same variety of goldfish. Surprisingly, he could identify males and females in the pet store. The Dinosaur visited the second store, and he could tell the difference here too. Does it mean that Dinosaur was right? That means all six fishes in his tank were female.

How is it possible?

The Biologist across the globe accepts many of their experiments as true at 95% confidence level. However, the Dinosaur saw a real-life example of how statistics failed. The Dinosaur decided to take few male fishes from the pet store. The Dinosaur also remembered an important lesson that he learned from this event:

The statistics can just tell you about the probability of occurrence of an event.

Hence it can be used as guidance.

However, there is a chance of error in statistics that is often neglected.

These small chances of error can sometimes have a very meaningful or disastrous impact.

Hence, we should never be overzealous to claim that something is perfect and there is no scope of error.

Even if someone is 99.99% confident, there is a 1 in 10,000 chance of failure of prediction/statistics.

The leader should be prepared to handle those 1 in 10,000 events.

8.2 Real-Life Management Lesson 8

It is not unusual to find managers that are overzealous about their experiences. It is not bad to be confident, but it may hurt one in the long run if one is overconfident. I knew many researchers who thought one event must occur if another is true. It is perfectly applicable to many cases. However, it may sometimes become a limitation in life. If one wants to achieve something unconventional, then you must look for something beyond the convention. It is almost impossible to achieve something big within the boundaries of comfort limit.

Being overconfident about past knowledge or training many times leads to a waste of resources and time. I know researchers who failed because they were overconfident about their past training resulting in wasting years for something that has no value for them or human society. There are also similar examples in various industries. A cosmetic company had a great philosophy. I appreciate their social responsibilities and corporate philosophy as they promoted gender equality and truly believed in women's empowerment. I came to know about this company first in 2013 while having a discussion with a friend who has a great understanding of the corporate world. At that time, we reached a conclusion, that the marketing strategy of the firm was excellent for the 19th and 20th centuries but may not be an appropriate strategy for the 21st century. Even though they had great products, their revenue started declining. After approximately four years from our discussion, I believe that we were right at that time. Probably managers in this company think that the company survived with the same marketing strategy for 140 years, therefore, it must survive with the same strategy for another 140 years. What they failed to notice was a changing world. I would like to quote Mr. John F. Kennedy here:

"Change is the law of life. And those who look only to the past or present are certain to miss the future."

The quote from Mr. John F. Kennedy applies to almost everything. Again, confidence is a great asset, but a leader should never be overconfident about their past experiences and statistics. Even though small, we should never completely neglect the chances of error. Once someone ignores the chances of error, that person/organization will not put effort to minimize those chances. It will lead to even higher chances of error. In my view:

CHANGE is the only law of life that does not have an exception.

Those who want to be a leader should always be prepared for the CHANGE.

8.3 Fun Facts From Chapter 8

Breeding fishes is the hardest part of having an aquarium. Many amateur aquarists think that putting multiple fishes together is enough to make them breed. The fishes can give birth to babies or lay eggs depending on the variety (species). The mollies and guppies are two freshwater fish varieties that are easiest to breed as they give birth to young offspring. The egg-laying fishes are harder to breed as they need extra care for their eggs.

Irrespective of whether a fish is a livebearer or egg-laying fish, there are few factors that must be considered. The temperature is a very critical factor as many fishes breed only in a particular season and temperature conditions for those seasons must be replicated in the tank. Another major factor is the number of plants in the tank. Fishes like to use the plants for multiple purposes. They can use it as a hiding place for them or their eggs or newborn.

The plants can sometimes act as an additional source of nutrition for fishes. However, the nutrition depends on the plant variety as well as the fish variety. Many fishes are very selective about the plants that they like to eat. Also, depending on the number and density of plants in the aquarium they can also act as a natural filter that controls the pH of the tank and minimizes the level of toxins such as ammonia and fish waste.

Replicating the natural environment of fishes is the best way to ensure that the fishes will be comfortable to breed. Live plants are one of the critical factors in creating the natural environment. In the absence of live plants, the aquarists can utilize plastic plants and other ornaments. However, the care required for breeding gets further complicated in the absence of live plants. There are many species of plants that multiply very fast in aquariums. They can be purchased at very economic prices in pet stores. One of my friends added two fishes to a completely planted aquarium that he had maintained for several months. He did not check the genders of fishes as he had no plan to breed them. Three months from the time he added the fishes, he found dozens of fish babies in the tank. Hence, fish breeding is not a very hard thing to do. The aquarists just need to prepare the right environment for them, and they will spontaneously breed.

9. TWO COOL WOLVES

One day the old Dinosaur went on a vacation. It was a long vacation that included travel to multiple geographical areas. The Dinosaur was interested in learning about different cultures. Hence, he planned to meet people from different cultures during this vacation.

One day, the Dinosaur traveled to a primitive tribe that lived in a jungle near a seashore. It was a tribe of wolves. It was a very interesting tribe. Even though they were disconnected from the rest of the world, they were very involved in learning. Culturally, they emphasized learning new things on regular basis. The Dinosaur felt that learning new things was like a ritual in this tribe where everyone gathered every month to share what new things they learned.

Interesting! Isn't it?

The Dinosaur got interested to learn about the reason behind the origin of this ritual. First, he asked a young person from the tribe about ritual. The youth astonishingly replied, “How come you do not know about this ritual? It should be common sense. God loves those who learn new things. You must be coming from an uncivilized society.”

The Dinosaur was good at dealing with criticism. He responded with a smile, “Indeed! You are right. I feel this is something my culture can learn from yours. I will try my best to take this message to my fellow dinosaurs.”

The youth was very happy about it.

The next day, the Dinosaur tried to find out one of the older people in the tribe. He found one who looked very wise wolf. The Dinosaur visited him and started talking about random things. The old Wolf offered Hookah to the Dinosaur. Both enjoyed the Hookah. The old Wolf asked about the life of the Dinosaur. The Dinosaur replied, “I am an old Dinosaur interested to know about different cultures. I will be leaving tomorrow for my next destination. However, I guess I could not learn few things about your tribe.”

The old Wolf asked, “What do you want to know?”.

The Dinosaur noticed the opportunity and queried about the *ritual of learning*. The Wolf looked intrigued first. Later he said, “It is a long story. However, I want you to promise that you will not share it with anybody in our tribe.”. The Dinosaur made the promise. The old Wolf continued the story.

Around 72 years ago, I was still growing up in the tribe. We were a tribe of almost 2000 happy wolves. We used to have a feast every night. We used to get fishes from the fisherman of the Lion King and enjoyed it every night. One day a traveler came to our tribe. He introduced himself as a 'Leopard'. The Leopard had traveled the world as a sailor and a part-time detective. He noticed that all the wolves were enjoying the fishes. We shared some fishes with him. He expressed gratitude and enjoyed the feast. He stayed with us for quite some time.

The old wolf suddenly became thoughtful and took a pause for few minutes. The Dinosaur respected the silence and kept enjoying the hookah looking at the beautiful blue ocean. Then the old wolf further continued his story.

One day, the Leopard looked at a fish and said "Guys! This fish is bad. You will get sick if you eat this fish." We were all naïve, nice & careless wolves. We expressed gratitude and avoided the specific fish. Leopard enjoyed the rest of the feast with all of us. Time passed by and every time the Leopard noticed a bad fish, he informed us about it, and we avoided that fish. It felt as if the Leopard had become a quality control officer. Before leopard joined us, some of us often had bad stomachs. However, Leopard came to the wolf community as a blessing. We never had a bad stomach after he came to our community.

The Leopard was a great person. However, he was getting old. One day, he got concerned about what will happen to the Wolves' tribe once he dies. After few days, the Leopard again noticed a bad fish. This time, he decided to change the approach. He called everyone in the tribe. Then, he said "Among all the fishes we got today from the fisherman, there is one bad fish. You all need to work together to find the bad fish. Then we can all enjoy the feast.

Surprisingly, it created a ruckus in the tribe. Looking at the unrest, the Leopard picked 7 fishes out of all the fishes. He kept those 7 fishes separately and said, "I want to make your life easier. One out of these seven fishes is bad. The rest of the fishes are good. Now, you need to identify bad fish. This way we will be able to enjoy feast sooner." Suddenly, several wolves came out ofthe group and claimed that none ofthe fishes are bad. They started blaming the Leopard. One of the wolves questioned Leopard's credentials. Another wolf asked Leopard to prove that the fish was bad.

The Leopard saved those seven fishes at colder temperature for 2-3 days. However, nothing changed. The wolves were still questioning the Leopard. Finally, the Leopard decided to teach the wolves. He discussed the criteria he uses to differentiate bad fish from all the good fishes. The Leopard expected the situation to improve after this session. However, few other wolves started blaming the Leopard for not helping them identify the bad fish earlier. One wolf claimed that he got stressed because of the Leopard and could not eat or drink anything for 2 days. There were a bunch of wiser wolves in the group. The wiser wolves thanked the Leopard for all the help he provided in the past. The wiser wolves also talked to other wolves who were baselessly blaming the old Leopard.

The tribe felt that the situation will improve after that day. However, two of the young wolves called themselves COOL wolves because they thought they were really cool. They decided to go to the Lion King to complain about the Leopard. The Lion King got concerned as the Leopard did not help other denizens of the Jungle.

The Lion King ordered the Leopard to meet him as soon as possible. The COOL wolves were very happy at the new development. The Leopard showed up a little late as he was one old LAZY Leopard. As soon as the Leopard entered the courtroom, he noticed the two COOL wolves and figures out what to expect.

The Lion King asked, "Mr. Leopard if you knew that one fish is bad, why you did not help other denizens of the Jungle in time?"

The Leopard responded, "Your majesty, approximately one year ago, I was discussing something with you. During that conversation, you told me that it is better to teach people how to fish rather than spoon-feeding them".

The Lion Kind said, "But that discussion is irrelevant here. Have you forgotten the rules of Jungle? We all live here peacefully and help each other whenever possible."

The Leopard responded, "Mr. King, I was just following your advice. I warned them about bad fish several times over the last few years. This time, I decided to teach them how to identify bad fish." The Leopard continued, "Your majesty, if you think it is wrong, I am still willing to repeat this mistake to make them independent in the future."

Being a wise king, the Lion King completely understood the situation. He thought for a moment and decided it would be useless to explain to wolves in royal ways. Hence, he requested Husky (the Advisor to Lion King) to handle the situation.

The Husky walked with the Leopard and the two COOL wolves to a meeting room. Once everyone was comfortable, Husky looked at Leopard and mischievously smiled. The Leopard reciprocated with a mischievous smile. The Husky next looked at the two COOL wolves and said, "You guys are really COOL, but some people try to be so cool that their IQ falls below room temperature." The Husky continued, "Nobody will know what I told you here. But next time, you are free to decide whether you prefer to be wise or stay COOL."

The two COOL wolves realized that they could have handled things in a better way. They never shared the story with anyone. The Husky, Leopard, and Lion King came up with the idea of the '*Ritual of learning*'. Over seven decades, it became a religious practice in our tribe. Now, if you ask people, they even have some legendary stories associated with the ritual.

The Dinosaur was amused. He said "*Life!". He took a big sigh and continued "At several moments, life gives you the options that were given to the COOL wolves. The choice is and always will be yours!"*

The Dinosaur started leaving and turned back to ask a question, "How do you know about this story or event if the two COOL wolves, Husky, and Leopard did not share this story?"

.

.

.

.

.

It was a moment of awkward silence!

.

.

.

.

The old Wolf responded with a mischievous smile, "Because, I am one of the two COOL wolves!".

.

.

Looking at the ocean he continued. "Probably, we all are!"

Life at several moments will give you the same options that were given to the COOL wolves.

The choice is and always will be yours!"

10. CONCLUSION

This world is an amazing

accident (for an atheist)

or

creation (for a believer)

that presents us with numerous opportunities to learn every day.

All we need is a curious mind and a playful heart that can read the encyclopedia kept in this global observatory.

As people grow, they somehow willingly or unwillingly become resistant to learning new things. They reject new ideas that do not confirm their beliefs. It is not unusual to hear someone claiming that they do not need to learn from juniors because they are working in a particular field from the time when the junior members of the team did not even start going to school. Probably a 10-year-old learns new things at a way faster rate than a person 3-4 times that age.

This resistance to learning hurts the individual as well as the organization. There have been instances where the managers/superiors laughed at the idea of a junior member of the team, but that idea later turned out to be a gem. If those superiors would have kept an open mind, they could probably become part of the success story. In another way, they could probably avoid the waste of time and resources related to the failures that could be avoided by the idea.

Learning is an art that is passionately pursued by a selected few.

Those selected few become the leader in the future. If someone has a curious mind, they can utilize their curiosity to learn something from every living thing on the planet or probably every object in the universe. I believe that the planet becomes an encyclopedia, and the universe becomes an observatory for those who are passionate about learning new things.

Learning is an art that is passionately pursued by a selected few.

11. WHAT IS NEXT?

Wait!

Think for a moment why this page is blank.

This blank page will tell you a story.

Once you know the story,

you can move to the next page.

If you came to this page without thinking,

then I give you another chance to think about a story

or

imagine a story narrated by this blank page.

If you have thought about the story, you are probably a leader or you have the qualities to be a leader. If you did not bother to think about it, then you could be a manager, or you may become a manager, but you must work hard to become a leader.

I know people who read hundreds of books every year that are related to leadership and management. Surprisingly, it does not make any difference for them. Therefore, I decided to write the leadership lessons in a way that kids and adolescents can enjoy. Kids and adolescents are active learners, and they are open to accepting new unconventional lessons. If you know any kid or adolescent, then you can give this book as well as other leadership books to them. I do not discourage adults from reading this book. However, reading books will only help adults if they are ready to implement the lessons in their lives.

Just reading a book and keeping all the information in the brain without implementing it will not make anyone better than a library with a collection of all the books in the world that cannot be accessed by any human being. This library cannot be used by anyone as it is inaccessible. Also, the library cannot make discoveries and change lives on its own. The aforementioned library can do no good to society unless it becomes accessible to people and people start utilizing the information available in the library to plan and implement a different future. In short:

Life is like a blank page.

The leaders try to fill this blank page by trying to do something unconventional that can become a leadership lesson for someone else.

AFTERWORD

This book is a newer version of an older book written by the author that needed some editing. I also added a new story that I created after publishing the first version. Hence, it is getting republished after editing with a new story. To avoid confusion, the name of the book is unchanged from the previous version.

I will be grateful if you can write a review of this book. Please be honest with your comments as they will help us improve our future content.

If you want a free copy of this e-book, please feel free to directly message the author on following the Twitter page or simply follow the social media accounts as all free promotions will be posted at:

Twitter: @MortiMiscellany
https://twitter.com/MortiMiscellany

Instagram: @MortiMiscellany
https://www.instagram.com/MortiMiscellany

ABOUT THE AUTHOR

Morti Miscellany

'Morti Miscellany' is a pen name used by the author of this book. The author is a Ph.D. with an interest in human behavior, learning, management skills, meditation practices, and health sciences.

Apart from his career in medical research and clinical duties, the author is passionate about travel-

ing, understanding new cultures, interacting with a variety of pets/animals. The author also helped his colleagues by facilitating meditation as a tool for stress management, anxiety management, and controlling burnout. The author is currently writing a book based on different meditation practices along with their benefits for individuals affected with certain conditions.
Please feel free to communicate with the author or follow for future updates using the following social media platforms:

Twitter: @MortiMiscellany
https://twitter.com/MortiMiscellany

Instagram: @MortiMiscellany
https://www.instagram.com/MortiMiscellany

www.ingramcontent.com/pod-product-compliance
Lightning Source LLC
LaVergne TN
LVHW050320160826
845677LV00014B/3500

* 9 7 9 8 7 1 5 7 0 0 2 5 4 *